Hodge the Hedgehog

Written by
Amy Sparkes

Illustrated by
Benji Davies

meadowside 🍃
CHILDREN'S BOOKS

Hodge the Hedgehog
hogged the hedge,
he didn't like to share.

KeeP OUT!

The other creatures
thought him rude,
but Hodge just did
not care.

Night and day
Hodge hogged away,
his nerves were
right on edge!

Hodge guarded his door,
to make quite sure
none came in his hedge.

His eyelids drooped,
his shoulders stooped,
Hodge could not go on.
He thought it best
to take a rest... but who
should come along?

It was a grey Mouse,
in search of a house,
and he stopped at
Hodge's door.

"What a fine hedge!"
he declared from the edge.
"Is there room inside
for one more?"

"Why should I share?"
huffed Hodge, with a glare.
"Hogging's what hedgehog's
are for...

...now I must go to bed,"
poor hogger Hodge said
and he shooed Mouse
away from the door.

But while Hodge slept...

...Mouse softly crept
to peep inside the hedge.

"What a huge place,
there's so much space!
How odd that Hodge
hogs at the edge."

"Poor Hodge must be lonely," said Mouse, "and if only he realised that sharing is fun..."

...then he had an idea,
"I could make
it nice here,
but how will I get
it all done?"

So he called Marvin Mole...

...who told
Vernon
Vole,
who
passed
on the
news
to Bill...

...who told
Harry **Hare**
the others
were there,
and the
hedge-house
began
to fill!

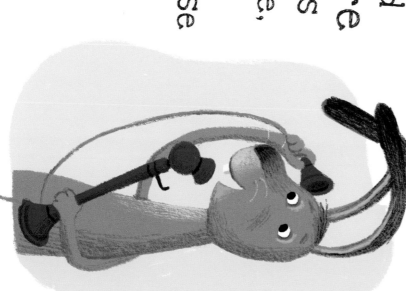

One by one,
they joined in the fun,
and still Hodge
made no sound...

...they polished and rubbed,
and painted and scrubbed
and hung pictures
all around.

They swept Hodge's floor,
mended his door
and cleaned his
plates and cups,

and last, but not least,
they prepared a fine feast,
and then woke Hodge Hedgehog up.

"My hedge!" Hodge cried, when he saw them inside, and he haughtily huffed at each one.

But after a while,
he gave a **big smile**,
when he saw all the work
that they'd done.

For to have them inside
was quite nice he decided,
perhaps his hedge hogging
was **wrong?**

Hodge
Hedgehog agreed,
it was time indeed,
for his Hodge-hogger
days to end.

...and Hodge never hedge-hogged again!

For Aidan
A.S.

For Frater Emmet
B.D.

First published in 2009
by Meadowside Children's Books
185 Fleet street London EC4A 2HS
www.meadowsidebooks.com

Text © Amy Sparkes
Illustrations © Benji Davies
The rights of Amy Sparkes and Benji Davies
to be identified as the author and illustrator
of this work have been asserted by them
in accordance with the Copyright,
Designs and Patents Act, 1988

A CIP catalogue record for this book
is available from the British Library

10 9 8 7 6 5 4 3 2 1

Printed in Indonesia